ROYALLY BAD

Billionaire. Playboy. Prince. My new boss.

Theo Kensington the most eligible—or ineligible—bachelor in the entire world. So what he's starred in a sex tape... or three? He's heir to the Kensington fortune. Son of a long lost Swedish princess. That's right—this tall, dark, and tattooed stud is a *prince*.

Except the queen pretends he doesn't exist. And the Kensington board of directors wants him gone.

Enter me. Vesper Smith, media consultant. AKA fixer. I have four days to convince this bad boy to behave. Clean up his image, clean up his act.

But this playboy prince is more interested in misbehaving. And if I'm not careful, there'll be a new costar in his next scandal: me.

ROYALLY BAD

LEE SAVINO

1

"He has a dick the size of the Empire State building —and an ego to match." The blonde on screen says with a perfectly arched eyebrow. The gossip newscaster across from her nods.

I hit pause and the video stops just as the blonde leans forward to impart another juicy secret about Theodore Kensington's dick. Her boobs look like they're going to topple out of her shiny pink blouse.

"Someone's already got a book deal to kiss-and-tell," I murmur to the frozen blonde on my phone screen. "No way you came up with that line on your own."

I press play again, bracing myself for more drama. I shift to ease the pinch of my high heels. This fancy marble porch isn't helping my feet any. I've been up since five a.m. to dress and check out of the hotel, and take a cab to this modern palace north of New York City. The driver had just pulled through the opulent gates when my Google feed started going nuts. I always set up a news alert so I can stay up-to-date with what the media is saying about my public relations clients.

"Theo Kensington has a long history of loving and leaving a trail of broken hearts. He's the son of a Swedish princess and an American businessman. Heir to the Kensington fortune. Kensington, Inc. alone is valued at $400 billion."

"He has incredible... assets," the blonde cackles.

"He's actually a prince, right?"

"That's right. But he doesn't like to talk about it. Prince or not, doesn't matter. In the bedroom, he's a god."

I pause the video again. The blonde on screen isn't the first to call Theo Kensington a god. Last year, a popular Hollywood darling tweeted, "Prince in the streets, god in the sheets," accompanied by a picture of the 'god' in her bedroom. A very naked god. The tweet was deleted, but not after it got seven thousand likes and retweets.

And now he's in the media again. Prince or god, he's my new PR nightmare.

I pocket my phone and ring the doorbell again, but I'm not surprised no one is here to greet me. Mr. Kensington's staff is probably watching the same media channels I am.

A shadow rises in the stained glass on either side of the door, and then the lock clicks open. A bear of a man with a shaved head and muscles straining his button-down shirt stands in the doorway.

Mr. Evans, head of security for Theodore Kensington.

"Have you seen it?" Evans says without preamble. "The sex tape?"

"Yes, I was just watching the interview..." I rewind what he said. "Wait, there's a second sex tape? Another one?"

"Just hit this morning."

Shit. I fumble with my phone. "I thought they were referring to the last one, the one with the porn star," I wrack my brain for the name of the blonde in the interview. "Pepper something."

"Pepper Spice. And no. This is a new one. A redhead. At least, I think that's what she is. She's not too clear in the video. Mr. Kensington, however…"

"Shit." This time I say it out loud.

"Exactly," Evans answers, grim-faced. He leans down and picks up my suitcase. "Normally I'd let you get settled in but—"

"We need to get ahead of this," I interrupt. "Where is—"

A bright orange Maserati roars down the drive. Bass on full blast, it zooms around the fountain accompanied by Metallica and squeals of delight. The air shudders as the car slides to a stop.

Three ladies trip out of the convertible, laughing. Sleek hair, huge boobs, and tiny handbags. They barely look at us as they head down a manicured walkway towards the pool.

A dark-haired man unfolds from the car, heavy metal still blasting from the stereo like a theme song. He doesn't bother to turn off the car, or shut the door before he tosses the keys to Evans, who catches them with a blank expression.

"Park it out back for me, Evans? Thanks, man," the new arrival says, and turns his smirk on me. I recognize him right away—the gorgeous, tanned face from this morning's tabloids.

Theo Kensington. Billionaire. Playboy. Prince.

My new boss.

He's not wearing a shirt. He. Is. Not. Wearing. A. Shirt. Who joyrides around the North Shore on a Wednesday morning without a shirt?

Prince Theo, that's who.

He strolls closer, chest muscles flexing. His muscles aren't the only yummy thing about him. He's got the best of his Nordic mother and striking father, perfect bone structure and bronze skin. Heavy brows over come-to-bed blue eyes. Black lashes long and thick enough to make any woman jealous. There isn't an adjective good enough to describe a man as pretty as him. Even the tattoos slinking up and down his torso and wrapping around most of his right arm don't detract from his prettiness. A panther tattoo prowls down his hip, disappearing beneath the waistband of his pants.

"Hey, babe," Theo says to me with a smile aimed to melt all the panties in the vicinity. Or maybe just mine. I'm pretty sure Theo's lady friends aren't wearing any.

My eyes hit the sleek V etched into his lower torso that leads to his groin. My girl parts roar to life like the engine of a Maserati. A smooth sleek purr, right between my thighs.

Shit. Ten minutes on the job, and I'm making eyes at my boss. Never mind he's the most eligible—or ineligible—bachelor on the East Coast... probably the entire world. Theo Kensington isn't a guy you take home to your parents. He's the guy you take to bed and gossip about him with your girlfriends after, in hushed, reverent tones, as the fuck of your life.

Or, like a bottle-blonde hussy with a book deal on today's entertainment news, tell the whole fucking world.

"Mr. Kensington." I extend my hand. He ignores it, and moves in closer. I'm wearing my tallest, most professional pumps and Theo still towers over me. There's an intensity about him, a hungry energy, some sort of powerful force field that would drag off my panties if they hadn't already melted.

No wonder all these women go to bed with him. No wonder celebrities star in his private sex tapes.

No wonder the board of his father's company wants him gone.

"I'm Vesper Smith," I withdraw my hand, because he's too busy undressing me with his eyes to shake it. "Your new media consultant."

"Nice," he drawls to my boobs. "I'm looking forward to you working under me."

I stiffen. I know I look good. I'm wearing a grey business suit that sets off my eyes, even hidden behind black-framed glasses. My heels make my legs look killer and give me a few inches of extra height. I look good, not slutty, yet my new boss is looking me up and down like I'm a pin-up model and he'd like to nail me on the hood of his car.

My heart sinks a little. He really is a man-whore.

I push my glasses up my nose. "Mr. Kensington," I start in my sternest voice. "You've cultivated quite the reputation. If you're not careful—"

Theo interrupts. "Where'd you dig this one up, Evans?"

The music cuts off as Evans turns the key in the Maserati. "She comes highly recommended, Mr. Kensington."

"Great. Do you want me to call the ladies back?" He jerks a thumb and I realize he's talking about the three women that just got out of the car. "We can do a photo shoot here. Something for you to put on Instagram."

He thinks I'm going to manage his Instagram account. "Actually, we have more pressing matters at hand. We need to prepare a statement, tell our side of the story. Pepper Spice already has a media tour—" I stop when he waves a hand in my face.

"Boring. You're hot, but you talk like my father's friends."

"That's who hired her," Evans said. "They're concerned that when the board next convenes, the vote won't be in your favor."

Theo shrugs.

I frown. "You're going to lose your seat on the board of a billion-dollar company and you're not even going to—"

"I need to get to the pool," Theo interrupts. "Got some friends waiting for me." He looks me up and down, and once again I feel that force field pulling me forward, clouding my mind, making me want to take off my clothes and make poor choices. "You're welcome to join me... if you wear a bikini." With a wink, he strides off.

I whirl on my heel to face Evans. "Show me the sex tape. Then I'll go down to the pool. Mr. Kensington and I are going to have a little chat."

Evans leads me down the mansion's wide halls, past giant paintings of landscapes and shipwrecks and Bacchus leading a party of nymphs and satyrs out to have a drunken orgy in a pasture. There's also a few statues, including a pink marble representation of Venus De Milo.

"Who decorated this place?" I ask.

"The late Mr. Kensington hired a collector who chose these pieces."

I tiptoe past the naked form. "Theodore Kensington's father was Turkish, right? An immigrant?" I had to dig for that information. Mr. Kensington the elder didn't want his immigrant status well known.

"Immigrant turned billionaire tycoon," Evans confirms. "Who fell in love with a princess."

"Kensington doesn't sound very Turkish."

"He changed his last name when he received his citizenship."

"Like Donald Trump's grandfather, changing the family name from Drumpf to something more marketable."

"Exactly." I don't miss Evans' dry tone as he turns into a small dark room. Empty coffee cups litter the desk under the many mounted screens. A pair of security guards nod as Evans introduces me.

"So you're the fixer," one says. "You gonna fix him?" The guard points to the screen where Theo stretches and poses on a diving board in front of an audience of bikini clad woman. One is already topless. The second security guard has the camera zoomed in on her.

"I'll do my best," I say as Evans hands me a laptop. He guides me to a private corner and gives me headphones. I pull off my suit jacket and press play. Theo's muscled chest and bikini wearing babes cavort on the big screen as I focus on the similar shadowy figures on small screen on my lap. I feel like I've got my own private peepshow.

Business as usual.

I don't know how I ended up the world expert on fixing sex scandals, but after five consecutive cases—three sports stars accused of sexual harassment, one philandering senator, and one startup CEO who dropped trou at a wild party a week before his company went public—I have a reputation. *Vesper Smith makes the bad boys good again.* That headline was on HuffPost last month.

Yes, I read my own press.

I have to say, of all the sex tapes I've seen, Theo Kensington's is the best. He's got a beautiful, muscled back that flexes with his buttocks in time with his thrusts. His jaw clenches and his eyes bore into the mirror over the bed. It's almost as if he's looking at me.

Then he pulls out and I get a good look at him. All ten inches.

The tape ends. I watch it again, feeling each thrust deep in my womb.

"So what do we do?" Evans asks when the grunting and squealing on screen has stopped for the second time.

I blow out my breath, and hope no one notices my nipples are hard under my blouse.

"It's bad, isn't it?" Evans says.

"It's bad, but not impossible. We need to give the media a new story: 'The Playboy Prince reformed.'" I hold up my hands and sketch air quotes. "He sowed his wild oats but he's ready to move on. Boys will be boys, the whole bit. It's sexist, but the media buys it. A year of him acting like a monk, doing charity work, and most importantly, staying out of the scandal papers will do wonders for him. He'll need to keep his shirt on." I straighten my glasses and look up at Evans. He's got his arms folded across his beefy chest, and looks skeptical. "It'll work. I know what I'm doing."

"I know," Evans said. "That's why we hired you."

"Okay, so we start scheduling events. First a public apology. Then some donations to charity, a few popups at society dinners." I nod. It all unfolds in my head: Theo suave and clean, the tattoos hidden safely away under a suit. I know this playbook—redeeming the bad boy. I got this.

"Sounds great," Evans says. "It's just what he needs. But it's not going to work."

"What's the problem?"

"We don't have a year."

"Hmmm," I tap a pen against my lips. "We can work with a shorter timeline."

"We have a week."

"A week!"

"That's when he goes before the board. That's when they decide. And that's not all." He hesitates. "There's the matter of the queen. Rumor is, she's finally asking about her grandson, and she's not liking what she hears."

"The queen? As in, the queen of Sweden."

"Yes."

"I didn't even know Sweden still had a queen."

"Their Parliament holds all the power, much like in England. But the queen is still an important figure. And her daughter was Mr. Kensington's mother."

"Estranged daughter," I correct. On this, at least, I've done my homework. "She left home at twenty, went to university in New York and dropped out. Fell in love with an up and coming businessman. From what I understand, Mr. Kensington only had five hotels back then."

Evans nods.

"The princess gets pregnant, they marry, the queen finds out and cuts her off," I tick off the rest of the story.

"Only to regret it when her daughter dies of complications in childbirth."

"Leaving an infant son and a mogul with a broken heart." I shake my head. "That has to hurt."

Evans scoffs. "If it did, the queen didn't show it. She hasn't even met her grandson."

"I didn't mean her. I meant Theo—Mr. Kensington the younger." I fall back slowly in my chair. Only child, now orphaned, shunned by his royal family. Kept from his rightful... throne? Did they still have thrones? "All right. I can work with this." Mentally I flip through my contacts. I can do this. Pull favors. Plan photo ops. "I can do a week."

"There's still a problem," Evans says. "He won't do it."

My head is still spinning from thinking about turning a tattooed, filthy-rich bad boy into a suave socialite with the innocence of a choirboy overnight. "Won't do what?"

"Any of it. The apology, the charity gigs." Evans shakes his head. "Mr. Kensington doesn't want to clean up his act. A few of the board members were friends of his father. They hired you to save his reputation, so they can give him one last chance. But he doesn't care."

"Then he needs a therapist, not a fixer." I say sharply.

Evans shrugs. "For the money we're paying you, you can be both."

3

On my way to the pool, I school my face into a stern expression, one I often saw employed by Ms. Mavery, the librarian at my high school. I found it works on handsy boys and misbehaving clients alike. Combined with my business suit and unflappable poise, I will be unstoppable.

I hope.

I follow the sound of classic rock to the pool. My polished approach is spoiled somewhat when my heel catches in a crack of the pavement. By the time I free myself, the whole party is staring—a handful of men and twice as many women. And Theo, who is still not wearing a shirt.

"You're fired," he shouts as I come close. The ladies around him erupt into laughter.

I continue down the marble steps, passing topiaries and statues of cavorting nymphs. I'm sensing a theme here. Maybe living among all this lascivious art made Theodore Kensington subconsciously decide to be a modern-day Bacchus. I smile to myself. "Art and the Playboy Psyche" would make a great thesis paper. Miss Mavery would love it.

"I said you're fired," he repeats, and there's a serious edge to his voice. This isn't just Theo, the bad boy idiot, playing to the crowd. This is Theodore Kensington, testing me to see what I will do. Whether I can stand up for myself.

"You can't fire me." I come to a stop before his pool lounger. "I don't represent you. I represent your dick." I point to his swim shorts. Fortunately, he's wearing shorts. Otherwise it'd be halfway to an orgy around here. I don't think Mr. Evans would like that.

"My dick can speak for itself," Theo says, and sets off another round of giggles.

"It certainly can. That's your problem. Your dick is getting rave reviews on entertainment news shows. Apparently, it just delivered the performance of a lifetime. You're a grown man," I'm full on channeling Ms. Mavery here, "who got caught with his pants down and more than just your hand in the cookie jar."

Theo wears a half-smile. There's a gleam of intelligence behind his model looks. *Thank God. Give me something I can work with.* "So I've got a PR problem."

"Mr. Kensington, you are the PR problem." *You and your harem.* Besides the three women I saw climb out of the car this morning, there are four more, all in the tiniest bikinis ever invented. They might as well be wearing thick pieces of string. And high heels. Who wears high heels with a bikini?

Theo cocks his head to his side. "What's your name, again?"

"Vesper Smith. Friends of your father hired me to clean up your image."

"I like my image just fine. You know what they call me?"

I cross my arms, making it clear I'm not going to say it.

"The god of fuck," he says. The ladies titter, but he's not

playing to his audience again. I've riled him. This show is for me. "You know why?"

"It's a play on your name. 'Theo', is the Greek root for 'deity.'" *Thank you, Ms. Mavery.*

Theo blinks.

The guy next to him bursts out laughing. "Theo, your new PR lady is a nerd."

"I'm drinking a martini," one of the ladies holds up her glass, "can you tell me the Greek root for that?"

I shake my head. Theo's groupies laugh and laugh, but he just studies me silently.

"Just how much Greek do you know?" a surfer looking dude asks me.

"Why the fuck do you care?" a woman with fire engine red nails, hair, and a bikini to match snaps at him.

"You know what Greek sex is, right?" He whispers in Red's ear, and she cackles.

I shake my head in disgust.

"No fucking way," Red points at me. "She's blushing like a virgin."

"Fuck," the first guy says. "A nerd and a virgin. I know someone who can help you with your V-card." He smacks Theo on the back.

"Lay off it, guys," he orders, before stepping close to me. Way, way up in my space.

My head tilts up to look him in the eye. I force myself not to back away.

"Your friends are jerks," I tell him.

"Don't listen to them. They've just never seen a media consultant as beautiful as you."

"I'm not going to sleep with you," I tell him. "Don't try to flatter me."

"Methinks the lady doth protest too much," he says, and

it's my turn to blink. "I think you like it. I think you want me to flatter you."

I push my glasses up my nose, more to insert space between me and him than to adjust my glasses. My hand almost brushes his tattooed pec. I wonder if he hears my heart pounding.

"You're a little uptight, Vesper Smith. Maybe my friend's right. You need a little Theo-therapy. Tell you what." He leans close, his lips brushing my ear. "You fix my image; I'll punch your V-card."

"That won't be necessary," I snap. He bursts out laughing.

"I'm kidding. I don't fuck virgins."

Screaming, "I'm not a virgin" won't gain me anything, so I spin on my heel and leave.

My cheeks are hot. Never mind the teasing. There's so much sexual attraction between Theo and me, the eye fucking alone is enough to get me pregnant.

Gods did that, right? Poof! Pregnant. Now that would be a story to spin. Mr. Evans wouldn't buy it, but every woman who'd been reeled in by that attraction beam would understand.

I glare at the naked statues of Greek gods as I march past. Evans meets me at the mansion door.

"We have a problem," he says. "I just got off the phone with Sweden."

"Did the queen see the news?"

"Yeah. She's finally ready to recognize her grandson."

"It's been almost thirty years. Why now?"

"I think she finally wants to make amends. She lifted the ban on her deceased daughter."

"A little late for that." Poor Theo, losing his mother at birth, and bearing the brunt of her sins.

"It's more a formality, to change the line of succession."

"What?"

"Her son is ill. He and his wife have no children. When he dies..."

"Theo is next in line," my head spins. "That's the real reason she's made contact."

"She's called him to an audience at her private residence. Friday."

"This Friday?"

"That's right. The queen wants to see him in four days."

"So how's it going?" My friend chirps. I wince, and prop my cell phone on my other ear.

I should be scouring my media contacts and calling in favors, and Googling what to wear to an audience with the queen of Sweden, but between Evans shouting about suing every woman his boss has ever slept with and Theo's heavy metal rock fest in his backyard, I have a headache.

I scowl at my suitcase. There is a bottle of aspirin in here somewhere.

"Hello? V?"

"One sec, Mina."

"You call me and then put me on hold?" She laughs.

"No, sorry. I just needed to find something." I pull the bottle of pain relievers from a secret pocket, and claw it open. Gulp down two, chase with water. Wish it was vodka and Valium. "Okay, ready. What was the question?"

"First day on the job? How's it going?"

Mina is my best friend, and the only person I don't lie to. "I want to quit."

"He's your client, right? Just fire him."

"I was hired to do a job. I'm going to do it," I say, and try not to grind my teeth. "I don't quit."

"Good for you. So, who is this guy again? What'd he do?"

"You've heard of the Imperial hotel chain?"

"The fancy hotels? Like the Four Seasons?"

"Exactly. My client's father started with one hotel, and built it up from there. Kensington, Inc. does a lot more now, they own other hotel chains, and an airline—"

"Bottom line, Daddy's boy has some serious cabbage."

"And some serious issues."

"What's his name?"

I sigh. "Theodore Kensington."

"Really? I just saw something about him..." I hear her tapping on her computer. "Oh, man. Oh, man." Laughter in her voice. I picture her scrolling through the pictures of Theo. A few photos of him with celebrity girlfriends, some on the red carpet, others taken by paparazzi stalkers. The camera loves Theo. Dazzling white smile amid the tan skin, the acres of muscles on his bare chest at the beach...

"Yeah."

"He's very photogenic."

"Mmmhmmm." *Wait for it.*

"Oh wow. Oh wow. Holy--"

"Yep. That's his dick."

"Looks like you have a big problem here. A really, really big... problem." She giggles.

"I know." I rub my forehead, wishing the pain meds would kick in. "I've never had a client's sex tape go live the day I start working for him."

"Aww, Vesper, you can pick 'em. So what are you going to do?"

"First I have to convince him to clean up his act. He's not interested in being anything but a bad boy."

"So? You like 'em bad."

"Not this bad." I tell her about his asshole behavior at the pool.

"Whew," she whistles. "He's like a boy in grade school, throwing rocks at the girl he likes."

"What? No."

"I'm serious! Sounds like the playboy prince has the hots for you."

I don't tell her the feeling is mutual.

"Listen, Mina, I was calling to see if you could look into something for me." Mina is a whiz on that computer of hers. Scary good. She pulls secrets for me all the time, and has helped me bury just as many.

I tell her what I need.

"I can do that. No problem. Just tell me this—"

"What?"

Mina's voice deepens to a purr. "Is he as hot in person as he looks on the screen?"

I grimace. I can't lie to my best friend. "Hotter."

"Fuck. You're totally screwed. At least, if you're lucky."

"Mina! I don't screw clients." *Not anymore.*

"More's the pity." Mina types faster on her computer, the sound like falling water. "All right. I'll get you what you need. You get your client on board."

"That's just it. I don't know how."

"You know how. Charm him."

"I don't do that anymore." I touch my glasses.

She laughs. I don't have secrets from Mina. "Not that way. But... there's nothing wrong with using a little bit of what God gave you to win him over to your side."

"No," I hiss into the phone. "No. I'm a professional. Just because I'm blonde, doesn't mean I'm a bimbo."

"You don't need to prove you've got brains, V. You got a

Bachelors and Masters from two top universities. No one is disputing that you're smart."

I pull off my glasses and give them a polish, waiting for a chance to interrupt.

"You've also got a great body," Mina continues. "Even if you don't flaunt it. You're not fooling anyone, hiding it under those suits. You are hot. There's no changing that. Why not own it?"

I drum my fingers against the windowsill. A few hundred yards away, Blondie slinks around the pool, walking like a model and a stripper combined. She's got Theo in her sights.

"You've got to charm him," Mina says. "or lose a client."

"I don't lose."

"Then you know what to do."

Once Mina hangs up, the pain in my head dulls to a resentful throb. I open the window a crack to get some air. Shouts of laughter waft up. The party is bigger. The music louder. The sun is hotter. It's a nice day. Gorgeous, in fact.

Fuck it.

Ten minutes later, I teeter past the nymph statues in my Louboutins. Before descending to the pool, I undo the tie on my wrap dress and shrug it off. Underneath, I wear a black bikini. A little more than the pieces of string the other women are wearing, but not much. I hang the dress on a statue, and walk on with only the swimsuit and heels.

Who wears high heels with a bikini?

Me, to reel in a client.

"V-card," Theo shouts from the diving board. The whole

crowd takes up the chant, bursting into applause when Theo dives into the deep end. I grin, wave, and grab a drink.

I stalk to the end of the pool to stand next to another white marble statue. This one's male, and well endowed. I toast him and his assets, and take a sip of liquor. *When in Rome...*

Two seconds later, Theo bursts from the water right in front of me. Water drips from his swarthy shoulders. His muscles bunch as he hauls himself out of the pool, and then he's walking toward me, rivulets running down the toned contours of his stomach. The panther tattoo snarls from his hip. That panther is on the prowl.

"Looking good. Still need to lose the glasses." He starts to reach for them and I shake my head, brushing his hand away. He gives me a panty-melting grin. "I guess the real party starts when they come off."

He's an asshole. He really is. But the way he says these awful things, tilting his head with just the slightest invitation in his eyes, I can't help but feel a rush of attraction. There are layers to his playboy act, as if he's seeing how much he can get away with. *I'm just fooling around;* his grin tells me. *Wanna fool around with me?*

Fuck, Vesper, you can pick them. I grip my glass tighter, give him a nod. "Mr. Kensington."

"Call me Theo."

All righty then. "Theo. Nice party you have here."

"Glad you could join us. I see you've given up on me."

"Nope," I say, and tip back my drink. I hold his gaze as I drink. When I set down the glass, he looks at me with new respect. *Finally.* "We need to talk."

"I like talking." He leans against the statue, angling so I'm sheltered by his body. We're in our own private world over here. My heart pitter patters. "I like doing other things, too."

"I know. I've seen what you like to do."

"Oh, you haven't seen everything."

"Is that so? Well, I've seen enough." I morph into Miss Mavery. "There's nothing wrong with a celebrity acting the fool. It's allowed, almost expected. But you're not a celebrity. You're the heir to a fortune and the son of a princess."

He half-sighs, half-groans, glancing back at the party behind us.

I lean into him to catch his attention.

"Your father built something from scratch and you're throwing it away. Usually it takes three generations to go from poverty to wealth back to poverty. You'll do it in two."

"I'm not going to have kids."

I take a deep breath. "Then there's the matter of your grandmother."

Theo's face goes blank, cold. The boyishness disappears completely, leaving an angry, bitter man. Still beautiful, though. "What about her?"

"She'd like to reconnect. She wants to—"

"No," he says.

"No? Let me get this straight. The queen of Sweden is summoning you for an audience, and you're going to blow her off?" I step close to him. One more step and my boobs would brush his chest. *Charm him.*

He shrugs.

"You're not even interested in finding out why she wants to meet you?"

He dips his head, nuzzles my shoulder. "There are other things I'm interested in." His lips brush my skin and set my body buzzing.

"So uptight," he murmurs. "You need a good orgasm. I can help with that."

"Maybe later," I say in a voice as brisk as I can make it, ignoring the fact that my libido has gone from zero to one hundred in three seconds.

"I'll hold you to that," Theo says, and the promise makes me shiver.

I clear my throat and press on. "Your uncle is sick. He might die, and that leaves you in the line for the throne. You'll be crown prince."

"I don't want to be a prince," he murmurs. His hot breath licks up my skin. "I'm already a god."

"You're not a god." I squeeze my arm between us, and push my glasses up my nose so I can give him a proper Mrs. Mavery glare. "You're a male Paris Hilton."

"Thank you," he smirks.

"Cut it out," I push at his chest. His rock hard, water slick chest that couldn't be more perfect if it was carved by Michelangelo. "This playboy act has to get old. Even I can tell you're smarter than this."

He straightens, studying me with eyes the color of espresso. "So what do you want me to do?" He sounds serious.

"We issue a statement condemning the sex tape as an invasion of privacy. Direct the press attention to your success and achievements."

"I don't have any of those."

"Your platform, then. You're the son of an immigrant who worked his way into the Forbes top 100 richest people in the world. You have a good chance of becoming the heir to the throne in Sweden." I try not to say it like I don't believe it, but it seems crazy. This tall, dark-haired, tattooed stud standing inappropriately in my space is a prince.

"You're going to be in the news for a long time, Theo. It's time to craft your message."

He blows out a breath. "All right."

"All right?"

"I'll do it. The interviews. The statement. Whatever."

"Really? You're sure?"

"Yeah, I'm sure. You convinced me. Does that surprise you?" He angles his head. Mine tilts opposite of his automatically. My chin goes up, raising my lips to his. "You are," his hot breath caresses my face, "very convincing." I close my eyes as a thrill goes through me.

"Theo!" One of the blondes calls, holding a margarita shaker. Somehow, she manages to simultaneously simper at Theo while giving me stink eye. "I have something for you." She opens the shaker and pours the icy, sticky liquid down her chest. Her nipples pop like fighter pilot buttons.

"Gotta go," Theo says, a wicked glint in his eye. He swaggers off, leaving me swaying.

I gotta go too, and craft a statement that will save my client's image. The conversation we had is a huge win. But as I listen to the happy squeals of blondie getting tequila licked off her skin by Theo's ready and willing tongue, I have to admit, it doesn't feel like one.

"WHAT THE HELL ARE YOU DOING?" Evans looks me up and down as I enter the mansion. I'm still in bikini and heels; I'd grabbed my dress but didn't have time to put it back on.

"My job," I answer, shrugging on my dress on and tying it up. "I've already crafted Theo's statement to the press. I just have to hit 'send.' My media contacts will take care of the rest.

Evans scowls. He's old school, hired by Theo's dad. He probably doesn't approve of media consultations done by the pool.

"You hired me to do a job," I defend myself. "I'm doing it. Theo—Mr. Kensington agreed to my course of action."

Evans blinks. "Really?"

"He's ready to clean up his image. I'm setting up a few interviews for him now. He promised he'd do them." *Right before he stuck his tongue in a woman's cleavage.*

"Is that so?" He touches the ear piece in his ears, listens for a moment, and then strides to the door.

"Where are you going?" I call after him.

"Mr. Kensington just left with his entire posse. Last time he did this, they almost burned down the Hampton residence."

"Shit," I breathe, and scramble to follow.

4

A hair-raising drive later, the orange Maserati pulls up to a curb, parking illegally. Evans motors up behind it.

I unpeel my fingers from the dash and seat. Theo drives like he's doing time trials for the Indie 500, and Evans stayed on his tail the whole way. The head of security must have tons of practice. And a judge in his pocket to pay off Theo's speeding tickets.

"Where are we?" The city block has nothing I recognize, besides a few rundown shops and a few ugly buildings amid a concrete jungle. We're north of Manhattan, a few streets over from the upper crust area, bleeding into a slightly seedy neighborhood.

"Skate park. Mr. Kensington bought the empty lot and had it put in, a month after he received his inheritance."

"Of course he did," I mutter, watching the tall, tanned figure leave the Maserati, skateboard under his arm. "Because he's twelve."

"I thought you broke through to him," Evans frowns at me.

"I thought I did too," I say, and head in. Theo drops his board to talk with a few guy friends who pulled up in a jeep. Soon they're all doing tricks, rolling up and down the concrete ramps.

To the right, a catering company has set up a long row of tables, covered in white tablecloths and mounds of food. Canapés and other finger food, plus a whole dessert table, with a tower of cupcakes. The women sit by and watch, careful to keep their sundresses from touching the gang tags on the concrete.

Theo flips his skateboard under his feet a few times before zooming up and down the ramps. He balances his big body with grace and ease as he executes some moves. He's actually good.

"Won a competition when he was sixteen," Evans tells me.

"Really? That might be useful." I make a note to get Mina to dig on that.

Evans stands up and signals his security team. "We have visitors."

Some scruffy kids have shown up, t-shirts untucked, jeans slouching. They hold beat up skateboards and eye the elite group who have encroached on their territory.

"Wait," I say. "They're like ten years old. Don't kick them out just yet."

A few of the boys creep towards the food table. When no one stops them, one grabs a chicken satay stick and runs back to his friends.

"Theo," one of the girls whines. "They're taking our food."

"It's all right," Theo waves. "They can have as much as they want."

"Stand down," Evans says into his ear piece.

The neighborhood kids swarm the tables. The caterers rush to bring out more plates. One of boys reaches over the sea of desserts and grabs the top cupcake.

"They're eating it all," blondie cries.

Theo looks up for a second. His shirt is off. Again. Tattoos in glorious display. He shrugs. "Let them eat cake."

Pouting, blondie stomps back to the car in her designer jean cutoffs and ridiculous high heels.

The kids demolish the food. Theo joins them for a mini hamburger, and then they all head over to the ramps.

I inch closer, listening to Theo rule the court, having the kids take turns on the ramps.

"Hey, can I borrow your phone?" I ask one boy. When he hands it over, I start snapping pictures. Theo crouching to examine a skateboard while three kids look over his shoulder. Theo pointing to the court, explaining the best way to hit the ramps. I take a little video and tweet it, adding Theo's most popular hashtag.

"What'd you do?" the kid next to me asks when I hand back his phone.

"Made you famous," I tell him. Using his phone versus mine will make the media leak look more authentic. "Some news vans are going to be here, and they'll want to talk to you. Go ask Theo if you can get a picture with him. If you can, I'll take it."

"Cool!"

Sure enough, thirty minutes later, the paparazzi show. Cameras flash. Theo poses with the kids. He trades his designer t-shirt for one of the boy's faded one. The boy glows. They all do tricks, and when one of the kids pulls off a fancy twist, Theo gives the boy his skateboard.

A few of the ladies get into it, handing out bottled water and the rest of the cupcakes. Blondie still sits glowering in the Maserati. I smirk at her before crossing to the news people to give a quote. This little detour has been quite a success.

When I return, Theo motions me over.

"Mr. Kensington?"

He pushes closer, dips his head towards mine. It's then I realize he's livid.

"What the fuck? You set me up."

I blink at him.

"It's a fucking media circus," he says. "Did you call the press?"

"No. I took a picture and tweeted it with your hashtag. You're hot right now."

"I'm always hot." Still flirty, under all his indignation.

"Hot news I mean." I flush. My stupid body senses his anger and thinks it's exciting. The chemistry between us cannot be denied. "You promised me a few interviews and then took off to here."

"Thought you would get the message."

"Did you expect me to give up so easily?"

"Yes." He pushes closer, and his scent washes over me. A bit of sweat at his temple turns his silky hair black.

"Well, I'm not going to." I stand my ground. "I'm going to do my job, like it or not. I'm a fixer. I'm used to difficult situations."

"I don't want to be fixed." He looms over me, his body heat hitting me like a heatwave.

"Well, too bad." My fucking pussy is dripping. We're so close to each other, you could barely run a knife blade between us. There's more to this fight than Theo's distaste for the media. He's finally met someone who will stand up to him. It doesn't hurt that I'm someone he wants to fuck.

"You used these kids as part of my own personal photo

shoot. And now I hear you told the media I come out here and skate with them regularly? A way of giving back?"

I shrug. "It's not a bad idea? You built the park, you like to come here."

"I'm not running a charity—"

"Actually, you are. As of three p.m. this afternoon. The lawyers are working on adding Boards for Boys and Girls to the Kensington Nonprofit Fund. You're giving one million to start a skateboard after school program for inner city kids." I give him a fierce smile. "I already told the kids you'd be here next week. Unless you want to back out..."

He shakes his head, but I hear his teeth grinding.

"Relax, Theo. This is good press. It's good."

"I didn't fucking come out here to—"

"I know you didn't. But, like I said, the kids showed up and you were nice to them. Because you're a nice guy." I poke him in the chest. It hurts my finger. His muscles are hard. Too late I realize I just poked my boss in the chest. But it's not my fault. The force field between us is activated.

I pull my hand away. "You're a nice guy," I repeat.

"No, I'm not." He backs away, shaking his head. He's even hotter when he's mad. I don't tell him that. "Don't pull this shit again."

"Mr. Kensington!" A man in a white polo and slacks jogs up. I practically jump between him and Theo.

"No interviews," I say, hoping Theo tones down the hostile body language before the cameras swing this way. That's all we need—Theo throwing a punch at a reporter. "Mr. Kensington isn't interested in giving a statement at this time."

"I'm not with the press." The man holds up his hands in mock defense. "I'm Roger White. I run the Kids Club over there." He points to a low, grey building alongside the park.

"I wanted to thank you all for coming and interacting with the kids."

"It was my pleasure," Theo says, shaking Mr. White's hand. All the anger has drained out of him. He stands tall and proud, inclining his head, as gracious as if he were the president accepting an award. "Thank you for the work you do. This afternoon was a drop in the bucket compared to that."

"I don't know about that. For example," he nods to two preteens who look like identical twins. "I've known Billy and Kenny since they were toddlers. Their mom works late, so they're in our programs every day. The older they get, the more they disengage. What you did today, it means a lot to them. And to me."

"Mr. Kensington has a non-profit that's interested in partnering with local kid's clubs," I put in.

Theo gives me a small frown, but doesn't correct me.

"I'd love to hear more," Mr. White says. "I know you're busy, but I'd like to invite you to the Kid's Olympics event we're having. Downtown. Clubs from the East Coast are all gathering together to compete. It's tomorrow. I know it's last minute notice to add to your schedule, but—"

"I'll see what I can do," Theo says, and thanks the man again while I grin in satisfaction.

"Theo," blondie hollers from the Maserati. "Can we go now?"

Theo ignores her, and takes my elbow, directing me to the car. The crazy attraction jumps between us again, making me almost stumble as I navigate the broken pavement to the black Escalade.

To anyone watching, he's escorting me to the car like a gentleman, moving his hand to my back to steady me. I feel the press of his fingers outlined on my back, burning like a brand. Like it's radioactive.

He puts his lips close to my ear. "What did I just tell you about posing for the press?"

"I didn't send him over to you." I whisper back, ignoring the crazy thumping in my heart. "That was all on Mr. White." I climb into the car and glance back, hoping to see the Theo who played with those kids. The real Theo, his gaze soft and open.

Instead he looks hard, shuttered.

I gulp and take a chance. "He's right you know. Mr. White. You did a good thing today. I'm sorry if I ruined it with the media." And I am sorry. *I thought the battle was between us and the press. Not between you and me.*

He stares at me so long I almost call his name. Blondie hollers again, and he shakes himself, breaking the spell. Thank God. Any longer and his force field would pull me from the car to jump straight into his arms.

"This isn't over," he warns and shuts the door while I shiver at the promise and the threat.

BACK AT THE MANSION, I head to my assigned office to check my laptop. There's an email from Mina with two words. "Mission Completed." I smile. Mina likes using code words as she executes her hacker genius.

My phone rings. Evans.

"I just got orders from Mr. Kensington. He said he's going to the Kid's Olympics tomorrow?"

I grin and thank the heavens above for Mr. White. "I guess so."

"He also asked for no extra media presence, but he says he's going to volunteer all day."

I fumble the phone and almost drop it. When I get it back up to my ear, Mr. Evans has continued, "—before flying out to Sweden."

"Has he agreed to Sweden?"

"Not yet."

"He will," I say, and knock on the wood top of my desk. I'll get him to agree to meet his grandmother the queen if I have to don a bikini and give Theo a lap dance.

I do not say this out loud to Evans.

"My men have been monitoring the media. Apparently, more sex tapes starring Pepper Spice have come out. She must have made one of every guy she's ever slept with. It's all over the celebrity news shows."

Well done, Mina. "That should deflect the attention from Theo somewhat."

"That's what I'm seeing." Evans clears his throat. "I don't know how you did it, but keep it up. We might be able to convince the board to give him a second chance, after all."

Four hours later, I close my laptop. I have Theo scheduled for an interview on Thursday, and released his statement asking for the press to "respect his privacy." I've nudged a few friends to lean on Pepper Spice, who's looking less and less like a credible source, and more like an opportunistic slut. I don't like dishing out dirt to clean up a client's image, but if Pepper is mud-slinging, the least I can do is turn the camera on her.

I've just finished dinner when my phone rings again.

"He's gone," Evans grunts.

"Again? I thought you took his keys?"

"I did. Must've taken the Porsche."

"The man owns ten cars. When you take his keys, you

need to take all of them." I stalk to the window and push open the shades, as if I expect to see Theo motor down his front drive. "We leave tomorrow at eight. We don't have time to pull him out of a bar and dry him out. We can't delay anymore. We're out of time."

"I know. We're trying to track his phone."

I whirl from the window, rubbing my temples. My headache was gone, but I feel it coming back with a vengeance. "Could he just be at the pool with the rest of his posse?"

"He sent them home. Thought he was headed to his rooms. We're searching the residence for him now."

Dammit. "All right. I'll help." I pack up my laptop and head to my room. If I'm going to run down my client, I'm going to do it in Nikes, not Louboutins.

I growl to myself as I march down the gilded halls. "God-damn fucking man better keep his fucking dick in his fuck god pants or I will staple them to his—" I open the door to my bedroom and halt in my tracks.

Across my bedroom, Theo grins at me.

My phone rings. I answer it.

"I think he's still here," Evans says, "His cell signal is still in the residence—"

"I found him," I interrupt. "Call off your search. We'll see you in the morning." I hang up before Evans can ask any more questions, and I have to tell him the playboy prince is lying in my bed.

5

"Miss me?" Theo asks.

"Shoes off the bed," I order, and march past him into the bathroom. With great care, I make sure not to slam the door. Then I press myself against it.

The sight of Theo, all shirtless six foot something of him —plus the ten inches he's packing in his pants (and thankfully, he is wearing pants) is enough to make my ovaries explode.

If I survive this night without rubbing myself all over him, I will be very, very surprised.

Must. Channel. Miss. Mavery.

I open the door again, half-hoping he's gone.

Nope. Still there, reclining on his back, biceps and triceps sleekly outlined against the bedspread as he pillows his head in his hands. He's kicked off his shoes. Looks like he's here to stay.

Some part of me is instantly resigned to him being here, our attraction as final and inexorable as gravity. Some part of me wants to jump his bones.

The way he's stretched out, it'd be so easy.

He transfers his gaze from the ceiling to me, long lashes fanning across his tanned skin.

How can a man be this pretty? And rich. And smart. And famous.

It's not fucking fair.

"So, Vesper. You gonna ask me why I'm here?"

"No," I reply, sifting through my suitcase for the baggiest pair of yoga pants I own. Add to them a giant t-shirt proclaiming 'I love NYC' and my Sarah Palin/Tina Fey black framed glasses, and I have the perfect cock-blocking outfit. Not as good as a pantsuit, but it's all I've got.

"I know what you're doing," I continue, rising with clothes in hand to kick off my heels. "You're making my life difficult. You've been doing it since I set foot on your doorstep."

"I agreed to do everything you wanted."

"Which is why I'm not throwing you out on your ass," I say. "You need a good night's sleep before tomorrow, and so do I. It may as well be here, where I can keep an eye on you."

"Is that what we're going to do?" He raises a brow. "Sleep?"

In answer, I shut the bathroom door. I wash my face and change into my armor. After I set my glasses on my nose, I study my reflection. I have a pretty face. Not as pretty as Theo's, but my thin build and elfin face get me enough stares on the subway. Add to that my long, thick blonde hair flowing out behind me like a golden flag, and I get more than second looks.

I've had enough attention to last a lifetime. But for some reason, I want Theo to look at me.

After a long moment, I let down my hair.

When I exit the bathroom, Theo sits up, and I know letting my hair down was a mistake.

But his hot gaze on me feels like a win.

"No, we're not just going to sleep," I announce. "We're going to talk."

"Just talk?" Another eyebrow raises.

"Just talk." I turn to the dresser to take out my earrings.

A whisper of fabric, and heat hits my back. Theo's awesome sexual presence surrounds me.

"Just talk? Are you sure about that?" he murmurs, wrapping his arm around my waist. A good thing he does, because my legs almost give out.

He pulls me back against him and my mind goes blank. Something long and very, very hard presses against my bottom.

"This is sexual harassment," the Miss Mavery part of me parrots. The rest of me melts into Theo's giant body.

"Is it? How so?" He tugs my shirt collar to the side and plants a small kiss on my shoulder.

It takes everything in me not to whirl around and wrap my arms around his neck. He's very hard and warm. And... hard. "Um..."

"Why don't you tell me all about it." He steps away and tugs me around. "In bed."

He draws me to the bed slowly. I walk very carefully, as if I might accidentally slip and fall and land on his dick.

Hey, it could happen. Baggy yoga pants non-withstanding.

But as soon as I get to the bed, I break away and slip under the covers. "No. Just no." I stop him when he goes to do the same.

He smirks and lies atop the comforter, propped on his side facing me. "You don't trust me at all, do you?"

"Not one bit, Mr. Fuck God. Your reputation precedes you. You made your bed. You can lie in it."

"As long as I can lie in it with you."

I roll my eyes. "Calm down, Casanova. You're not going to seduce me tonight."

He traces the design on the blanket, his finger straying dangerously close to my boob. "Can you blame me if I try? You're hot."

I give him a look.

"Oh, come on. Not even those glasses hide it. Though they do give me tons of sexy librarian fantasies."

"Your books are overdue, Mr. Kensington," I say sternly.

"Fuck me," he groans, rolling to his back.

"No. Not gonna happen. I don't fuck boys who are prettier than me."

"I'm not boy. I'm a man."

"Then act like one. Skateboarding? Really?"

"I like it. I won a competition—"

"When you were a teen. You're twenty-eight."

"How old are you?"

"None of your business."

His eyes glitter. "I can make it my business. I'll call down to Evans right now—"

"Twenty-six."

"You're young."

"Age is just a number. I've got experience."

He smirks.

"As a media specialist," I clarify. "My last five clients—"

"I know about your clients. I read your file."

"You read?" I snark back, and he makes a face.

I hit him with a pillow, and he grabs it from me, putting it behind his head.

This is nice. This is comfortable. At least, as comfortable

as we can be with all this sexual tension buzzing between us. The air is charged, like just before a storm.

"I guess your glasses make you look older. More... experienced."

I smile at this.

"So what made you want to be a fixer?" Theo asked.

"Everyone has secrets."

He tilts his head closer. "You gonna tell me yours?"

"What do you think?" I pull the sheet up under my chin.

"If you tell me yours, I'll tell you mine."

"Too late for that, Mr. Fuck God. Your dick is all over the internet. You don't have any secrets." I plump my own pillow, sink into it with a sigh. "Not that you've ever had much privacy. Billionaire, son of a princess. You've lived your whole life in the spotlight. Must get old."

"It does," he says softly, and there's a sad note in his voice, a hint of the man I saw before. Much older and more serious than the usual playboy the world knows. Soft and open, able to be hurt.

I might be the only one who's ever seen the real Theo.

"You're so beautiful," he says, and my heart stops. There's nothing flirtatious about his tone, none of the irresistible charm. He serious, stating a fact. But I am very aware of his hand resting on the bed between us, five inches from my hip. It would take nothing for him to slide it forward, to pull down the covers and find my bare skin under the baggy t-shirt. His touch wouldn't even be shocking. It wouldn't be wrong.

Us, lying together without touching, that is shocking. Being in bed with Theo feels inevitable.

It doesn't make it right.

I press my lips together and stare at the ceiling.

"When I first saw you, I thought you were, I don't know",

he shakes his head, "a model or something. A pretty face sent here to sell something. Then you opened your mouth and—"

"What? Beautiful women can't be smart?"

"I don't usually hang out with women because they're smart."

"Pepper Spice is smart. She turned one night with you into media attention and a book deal."

He says nothing.

"And I am a pretty face sent here to sell something," I continue. "I'm going to sell the world Theodore Kensington: fine, upstanding citizen. And you know what? It won't even be a lie."

"My whole life is a lie."

"What are you talking about? You live in a mansion in one of the most expensive neighborhoods in the world. This place is practically a palace."

"This? I hate this place. My father built it for my mother. Ten years after she died." He scoffs. "He never stopped loving her. Never stopped..."

"Trying to prove himself?"

"Yeah," his voice kicks with a mirthless laugh. "I guess so."

"So you had a hard childhood. That's not unusual."

"What about you?" He turns that deep gaze on me and I flick my own down. I want to shrink into myself, a hermit crab in a shell. *Don't look at me.*

But he does. There's no hiding from the dark blue depths of his gaze.

"Tell me something about yourself, Vesper Smith. Something real."

"Truth or dare?" I joke, and wish I could take it back. Theo lies on his side, his dark gaze soldered to my curves under the blanket. And I'm wet and ready, body just waiting for him to make the first move. At this point, a dare would be very, very dangerous.

I swallow. "I'm from a small town. Only child."

"Parents?" he probes, more intent than I've ever seen him. His sexy aura is turned way, way up. This close, it's overpowering.

"Just my mom. She worked a lot."

"So did my dad."

"Yeah, well, at least you weren't on food stamps." I grimace at the ceiling.

"So no modeling career?"

"No. Pretty girls in my town ended up at the strip club."

"What got you out?"

"Work, desire. A bit of luck. I had a teacher who believed in me. She was the school librarian. I befriended her. I thought all the books were hers. She was nice to me. She told me I could go to college, and I believed her."

"Did you go?"

"Bachelors and masters."

"Smart girl. Scholarships?"

"And loans. I also worked." I touch my glasses. "Got an internship with a fixer who taught me everything she knew. And here I am."

"In bed with me."

"This is not going on my resume."

He laughs, and I wriggle around to face him. The heat between our bodies is potent. Electricity leaps from his tanned skin to mine. Even covered in a white sheet, I can feel it.

I lick my lips. "You know what would make me very, very happy?"

"I think I can guess." The devil lurks in his grin.

I hold up a finger. "One interview. Prime time. I can make a call—"

"No." He jerks away from me, only a few inches, but I feel the wall go up between us.

"All right, then. How about this? The kids you met today, the ones going to the event tomorrow? Comp them some rooms. You own a hotel a few blocks away."

Now he's lying on his back staring at the ceiling and I'm leaning into him.

"It'd be a great gesture. It'd make their year. I promise not to leak it to the press. Although, it'd be great if you made an appearance. Just show up, make the kids feel special."

"Is it really good for these kids to be seen with me? My reputation..."

"You are not your sex life, although you've done a good job trying convince everyone that. But is that all you want to be? You're a fucking billionaire. I know it doesn't mean as much to you because you were born to it, but remember Billy and Kenny? Their mom works double shifts as a waitress at Denny's. Their father's in jail. You of all people know what it's like to have a parent working all the time, and one gone."

He flinches.

"You could make a difference in their lives, if you wanted to. You just have to get over yourself." I flop onto my back, rant over.

There's a long stretch of silence.

"I don't mean to ride your ass," I add. "I want you to realize the good you can do. It doesn't have to crimp your party life. Or sex life."

"You can ride my ass anytime."

I give up, rolling away from him and setting the alarm on my phone before turning off the light.

Behind me Theo shifts, and presses his body against mine, lining it up behind me.

His arm comes around, wrapping around me over the blanket.

My body is alive, holding its breath. I wait for him to pull me to him, to kiss me and do all manner of naughty things that would shock a porn star, not to mention Miss Mavery.

But he doesn't, so I fall asleep.

I JERK awake when my phone buzzes like an angry bee.

I grab it, squinting to check it. Three a.m.

"Do you have to keep that thing on?" Theo asks. In sleep he threaded his legs through mine, tangling us together.

I power the cell down, and let Theo take it and set it aside.

His cock probes me as I settle back. He says nothing more, but from his breathing I can tell he's wide awake.

"Theo?"

"Mmm?"

"Why didn't your grandmother want to meet you until now?" It's a blunt question, but the darkness softens it.

"I've always wondered that," his voice is muffled behind me. "My dad told me she hated him. Hated that her daughter ran away and abandoned everything she'd been raised to do.

So she shunned her own grandson? How sad.

"My dad went to work to prove himself. Built an empire. And then he died." Bitterness laces Theo's tone.

"I'm sorry. You deserve to have family." *You deserve to be loved.*

He holds me tighter, and I find his hand, stroke his wrist.

His fingers squeeze mine, and then slide downward.

"What are you doing?" His hand brushes my stomach, breaching my baggy t-shirt before slipping under my yoga pants. I hold my breath as he cups my hot, throbbing pussy.

"Theo—"

"Shhh," he mutters. "You need this." *I need this,* I hear his unspoken thought. Diverting from difficult emotions to promiscuous sex. Story of Theo's life.

At the moment, I don't care. His fingers stroke up and down, the lightest of touches. The coil of arousal tightens. I whimper and he delves deeper, soothing the ache even as he makes it worse.

This is a bad idea.

"No, it's a not," he says, and I realize I spoke aloud. "Let go. Let me take care of you."

I relax, all but my hips, which cant back and forth against his touch. His index finger finds the spot next to my clit and flicks it until I shift, restless. Pleasure builds in me, threatening to take over. It's too much. I want to shy away. Theo drapes his leg over mine, capturing me, keeping me still so my orgasm can catch me.

My climax blooms slowly, spreading through my breathless body, blanking my mind. Theo keeps up the light, fluttering touches until my inner muscles clench and spasm, begging for more.

I sigh and sink further into his body. *God in the sheets.*

"Thank you," I whisper, and he kisses the back of my neck.

"Go to sleep."

I do, wondering if I'll be able to keep Theo's dick out of the press—and my pants.

THE KID'S Olympics is at the stadium downtown. We leave the mansion at eight a.m., in a convoy of Escalades. Theo opted to ride with me. I frown at my phone the whole time, scrolling through newsfeeds, but I feel him watching.

The dirt on Pepper Spice Mina found yesterday has done its work, deflecting attention from Theo. Between his demure statement (crafted by me) and his positive photo op at the skate park, he's looking a lot better in the news. People are willing to forgive a rich, handsome guy and his sexual exploits a lot faster than they would anyone else.

Sexist, but it's true.

"We're here," Evans announces when we pull up to the stadium.

"No press," Theo mouths as we walk in, and I nod.

He accepts a complimentary volunteer shirt, and my hand itches to grab my phone, take a picture, and send it to my friend at *Good News, America.*

Instead, I accept a shirt as well, and plunge in.

The day whirls by. At one point, Evans calls me over to tell me the *Wall Street Journal* wants to do a write up of Theo's dad and Kensington, Inc. and they want a quote from Theo.

"Tell them we're preparing for an audience with the Queen, and that we'll have something to them by Friday." I can only hope Theo will commit to cleaning up his act by then. At least today he seems to be having fun. The kids flocking him don't bother him at all. Plenty of parents are here, too, and ask for pictures. Apparently, Theo's skateboarding prowess is enough to make him popular with the kids, and his status as a scandalous public figure—on level with the Kardashians—is enough to make him a minor celebrity with the adults.

And Theo? He just hangs out with the kids, and enjoys

himself. Biceps flexing as he lifts one up to make a slam dunk. Tattoos peeking out from under the volunteer shirt he wears. Sexy smile drawing yoga-pant wearing moms like flies to honey. And these women's yoga pants are skin tight.

"I thought you weren't doing pictures," I grouse to him at lunch.

"I said no press. I don't care if the kids want pictures." He offers me his water bottle. I shake my head and he caps it. "Why, you jealous?"

"No."

He throws an arm around me. I push at him, trying to get free, but he's too strong. His manly scent washes over me, sexy cologne mixed with the smell of the popcorn they sell at the stadium. He smells like a teenager on a first date.

My cheeks heat, remembering how he held me all night. And then gave me an orgasm.

"Hey," he calls to his new ten-year-old buddies. "Take a picture of us?"

"Theo—"

"Smile," he orders, so I do.

THEO HAS a limo pick up the Bronx kids to take them to the hotel. They're all wide smiles, brimming with excitement. Mr. White shakes Theo's hand, thanking him again.

"Come on, V-card," he murmurs, grabbing my hand. Energy zings up my arm, as if I've hit my funny bone. My body fills with a not quite painful ache.

In the backseat of our own limo, I lean into Theo, resting my head against his shoulder until my glasses dig into my face. I don't ever want to move. The white volunteer shirt sets off his tanned skin perfectly. I want to crawl into his lap and curl against his chest.

Instead, I distract myself with my phone, checking my social media sites, and because I'm on the clock, his public pages.

"Hey, look at this," I say, and show him his Lookbook page.

His hair tickles my skin as he leans closer. I clear my throat and scroll through all the pictures of him with the kids. There's one with him kneeling beside an adorable boy in a wheelchair. Theo's grin makes my heart ache.

"You're getting a lot of great comments," I say.

Theo squints at the screen. He plucks my glasses off my face before I can say anything, sets them on his nose. I open my mouth, but the black frames highlight his beauty and, for a second, I can't breathe. Nerd Theo is fucking hot.

Brow furrowed, he tries to read the screen before jerking his head back, pulling the glasses off and staring at them. "Vesper, these are—"

"Fake," I say, and give him a sheepish grin. "You caught me. Do you need glasses to read?"

"I don't read, remember?" He frowns at the glasses.

"You can though. You just won't. You avoid anything that makes you look responsible or smart."

"Is that why you wear these?" He offers me my frames. "Do you think they make you look smarter?"

"Maybe." I take them, turn them over in my hands. The black lines. The clear glass. It all seems so stupid now. I slip them into my purse with my phone.

"Why don't you tell your doctor you need glasses?" I ask Theo. "Or just get Lasik surgery?"

He slides away from me on the seat. "I told you. I don't read. I barely passed high school. Flunked out of college. It didn't interest me. What I don't understand is why you wear fake glasses. You don't need anything to make you look smart."

"I put myself through college," I blurt. "I worked at a bar. I got great tips."

"I bet you did."

"Theo..." I turn away. "Never mind."

He catches my hand. "No. Tell me."

"I kept my hair long. I was afraid to cut it in case I wouldn't get as much attention. Wouldn't make as much money." I realize I've pulled my ponytail over my shoulder, and am stroking it. I stop. "One day, a guy comes in. Big spender. I flirted with him. He told me he owned a club, and was looking for a new bartender. Offered me a job."

"Did you take it?"

"I went with him to his business in the big city. It was a club. Membership only—fifty-two thousand a year. Lots of girls in tiny dresses, and older men."

"Sugar babies with their sugar daddies."

"Yep," I swallow hard. "That's what people see when they look at me. Long legs, blonde hair. They think I could be a model, or a stripper, or..."

"That's not all they see." He finds the glasses and slides them back on my face. "Just because you're hot as fuck doesn't mean you're not intelligent."

That's not what people see.

"And look at you now. Vesper Smith. Fixer. You make the bad boys good again."

"I don't know about that."

"You're reforming me," he insists. "And later this week, you're gonna meet the queen of Sweden."

I still. "You're going?"

Theo shrugs. "Why not? She's just a person."

"She's your grandmother."

"Yeah, she's been a fantastic grandmother so far."

I put my hand on his knee. "Losing your mom must have hurt her."

"It hurt me too. My dad never recovered."

I wait, but he says no more. I move my hand from his knee. I should probably stop touching him so much.

But then he puts his hand on the back of my neck. Slowly pulls the hair band out, sifts his fingers through my hair. I close my eyes in pleasure.

"I like your hair. Though, I wouldn't mind if you cut it."

"Thank you."

"You better come to Sweden with me. You look more like Swedish royalty than I do."

"I don't know about that." I shift away from him to look out the window. We're almost to the hotel, the crown jewel in the Kensington portfolio. Fifty-two stories high, overlooking Central Park.

How did I end up here? I feel like an imposter.

"One interview," Theo says suddenly.

"What?" I pull my gaze from the park.

"I'll do one interview. Set my story straight. After that, I just want to stay out of the press."

"I can do that." I smile back and pull out my phone, ready to schedule the interview before he changes his mind.

My Google alert pings. I scroll through the latest news bulletin.

"Shit," I say.

"What?"

"Your uncle died," I tell him as the Escalade stops at the grand entrance to Imperial Manhattan. "Congratulations, Theo. You're now the crown prince of Sweden."

6

The door opens into the storm of paparazzi. Cameras flash like lightning. The press screams from all sides.

"Mr. Kensington," Evans shouts. Black suited men rush forward, surrounding us. Theo covers me with his body as we race inside.

"It's all over the news," Evans tells us.

"Fuck," Theo runs his hand through his hair. "I'm sick of this. What do we do?" He and Evans turn to me.

"You're the most newsworthy person on the planet right now. If you thought you were famous before..." I shake my head. "I'll release a statement announcing that you're grieving with the family. We'll head to Sweden early."

"What about the interview?" he asks.

"There's still time for one. I can get you on *Good News, America* tomorrow. Hell, I can get you on air anywhere we want. But I know Reba Hamilton," I name the head anchor. "She'd love to interview you, and she'll be nice. Classy."

"Let me think about it," Theo says.

"Let's get you into a secure location." Evans leads us to a private elevator. Fifty-two floors later, we step out into a penthouse suite. Black suits precede us, and a few more follow us in.

"We've tripled your security. Sweden is sending a liaison, also."

"Am I going to have to learn Swedish?" Theo jokes.

"Maybe," I say. "Polling says you're not very popular over there. I expect the queen will have a list of things she requires before you're officially named heir to the throne."

Theo sighs and runs his hand through his hair. He's still as gorgeous as ever, but there are little lines of strain around his long-lashed eyes. His strong shoulders slump a little. "Can I get some privacy? I'd like to consult with my media consultant."

"You all right, Prince Theo?" I say once the suits and Evans are gone.

"Don't call me that."

"You prefer My Liege?"

He smiles, prowling forward and all of a sudden, I have the playboy prince back. "I prefer to be a god."

I retreat, and he keeps coming until my back is against the wall. He puts a hand above my head and leans in. "In fact, that's what you'll be calling me tonight."

"In your dreams, skater boy," I duck under his arm and escape. "So, the interview. Did you change your mind?"

He's still at the wall, leaning against it, staring at nothing.

"Theo?"

"Have dinner with me." He straightens, but still doesn't look at me. His shoulders hunch slightly.

"What?"

He looks at me, and every muscle in me clenches with

need at the longing in his eyes. "Have dinner with me, Vesper."

"Why?" I whisper.

"Today, volunteering, did you have fun?"

"Um, I guess." His change of mood from sexy to serious is giving me whiplash. Almost like the real Theo is trying to break free, and seduce me at the same time.

"You looked like you were having fun."

"I did. I mean, all the people wanting pictures with you were annoying."

"Since when do you not want pictures of me? You just didn't like the hot moms."

"They were not hot moms," I burst out. "Those yoga pants were way too tight."

He grins at me.

"All right. I had fun."

"Have dinner with me. You can say it's for work. Get to know the real me."

"For work? Just a moment ago, you said you wanted me in your bed."

"I want you calling me a god. It doesn't have to be in bed."

I groan.

"Hey, you represent my dick as much as me. You may as well try it out."

"This is the weirdest conversation I've ever had." I throw up my hands. "Fine. You want dinner with me? Do the interview tomorrow."

"Sold," he says, and I realize I've been played.

Too late. He's going to the door, calling Evans back in. I spend the next few hours confirming the interview for tomorrow, crafting and issuing a statement, and debriefing Evans and Theo.

"Your private plane is on standby," Evans says. "We can fly out to Sweden whenever you're ready."

"Tomorrow night," I say. "Let's get to Stockholm and get over jet lag before the audience."

Theo nods, rubbing a hand over his face. He's changed out of his volunteer shirt, into a polo and shorts. Evans brought my bags by the penthouse so I could freshen up. I put on a dress, and send my suitcase to my room, hoping it's far away from Theo's. A few floors away, or better yet, across the street. Or country.

Sitting close to him, working together, the attraction has only grown. We're both tired. Not great for the self-control.

I stand and stretch, ignoring how Theo's eyes sweep over me. "One thing at a time. Let's focus on the interview. Reba sent me a list of preliminary questions we can work on. She'll be polite, but she won't hold back. We need to practice."

"All right," Theo says, and jumps up. "But first, dinner." He grabs my hand, pulling me to the door. "If you need us, Evans, we'll be at the pool." Evans' frown follows us, but there's nothing I can do.

THE POOL IS on the roof, a dazzling oasis complete with palm trees and a few fountains. I haven't really fought to get free from Theo's grip—a deal is a deal—but once we walk out into the luxurious space, only the sky above us, I tug my hand away.

"I have to make a call," I tell him.

"No problem." Theo tosses me a few pieces of string that supposed to be a bathing suit. "Do your thing, then change into this."

I sigh, and turn away.

"What's up?" Mina answers on the first ring.

"How's it going?"

"Looking good over here. Did some quick polls. U.S. populace loves the Prince thing. They seem mostly amused by the whole Pepper Spice scandal. Not sure about the board of directors—that might take some groveling."

"We're on it. The interview tomorrow will help."

"How is Prince Charming?"

"Still a domineering asshole." I grimace at the bikini I'm holding.

"I heard that," Theo shouts from the bar where he's pouring himself a drink.

Mina snickers. "He's in the room with you?"

I sigh. "We're doing dinner."

"Ho, boy. Somebody's gonna get royally fucked."

"No," I scoff. "We're working. Practicing for the interview tomorrow. This was the only way I could get him to do it."

"You keep telling yourself that. Sounds like a date to me."

"It's not a date—"

"Yes, it is," Theo hollers from across the pool. He's now seated at a little table set for two.

Mina guffaws and I roll my eyes. "Gotta go."

When I return from the changing room, bikini in place under my dress, the food is all served. Theo stands and helps me into my chair, the perfect gentleman.

The place is abandoned. Either no hotel guest has happened to come up here or Theo arranged for us to have privacy. I suspect the latter.

Theo lifts the cover off my plate, and the delicious smell hits my face. My stomach growls. We fall on the food.

"This is nice," I say after I've cleaned my plate. Volunteering all day is hard work. "When did your father build this hotel?"

"This is the hotel where my parents met."

"Seriously?"

He nods. He's been a little quiet through dinner, dark and brooding. Maybe this is why.

"You never talk about your parents."

"I didn't really know them." Theo dips a tiger shrimp in the sauce and holds it to my mouth. "Open."

I keep my mouth shut.

"You allergic?"

"No."

"Then trust me."

I let him feed me. "Oh my god," I moan. "Fuck, that's good."

"You have a dirty mouth for a girl," he says. "I like it."

"You're just plain dirty." I slurp down more shrimp. Usually I'm careful with how I eat, but tonight is surreal. I'm on top of the world, having dinner with a prince.

Not a prince. A god.

I giggle.

Theo raises a brow. "I'm going to make you slow down on the wine."

"I'd have thought you'd get me drunk so I'd end up in your bed."

"That's cheating," he says. "I'm a gentleman."

"Yes, you are," I say, trying not to sound surprised. "You are a gentleman."

"I always let the lady come first," he continues.

I groan. "You were doing so well. The beautiful setting, the food, keeping on your shirt..."

"What's wrong with me taking off my shirt?"

I press my hand to my forehead. "Do I have to answer that?"

"No," he says, and stands. With exaggerated slowness, peels off his shirt. I suck in a breath as the panther tattoo comes into view. My lady parts purr.

"Come on," he says, smiling like a cat with cream. "You gotta admit, this is a good look for me."

It is. It so is.

"No comment," I say, my head cocked to the side, studying his panther tattoo.

He takes my hand, pulling me from the table to poolside.

"Come on, V-card. Time to get wet. Unless you are already?"

"No comment," I laugh, and shrug out of my dress, shedding my inhibitions along with my clothes. I'm on top of the world, and I don't care what anyone thinks. Is this how Theo chooses to live his whole life? It's freeing.

"You're beautiful," Theo tells me.

"I know." I step past him and glide into the water.

He follows and we swim around each other in circles, in ever tightening loops until we're close enough to touch.

"How do I always end up half-naked around you?"

"You weren't half-naked last night."

"That was a fluke." I give him a Miss Mavery glare, even though I'm not wearing my glasses. "You were very, very bad."

"And you were very, very good. But I suspect the good girl is just an image. Come on, Vesper." He catches my hand, tugs me a little closer before I pull free. "Come be bad with me."

Need zings through me at his touch.

Fuck it.

"I'm already being bad. A date with my boss. Bad idea."

"I'm not your boss. I fired you, remember?"

"That's right. You did. You were and are a consummate asshole. So why would I want to date you again?"

"Because," he steps into my space and puts his hands on my hips. "I only fired you so I could do this."

He's going to kiss me. At the last moment I turn my head, and let him brush his lips on my shoulder. I shiver as he kisses up my neck.

"You're good at that," I tell him when he lifts his head. "Lots of practice?"

"Not as much as you might think," he says.

I raise a brow.

He backs away. running a nervous hand through his hair. "Fuck, Vesper. I know I'm a slut, but it's not as bad as it looks."

"Relax," I say. "I don't judge. I've slept with plenty of guys." *If you only knew.*

"And I know I was a jerk to you, in the beginning. I apologize."

"I accept. In grade school, the guys threw rocks when they liked me. I can handle cocky behavior. Although... I should tell you a secret," I lean in to whisper. "I'm kinda attracted to jerks."

"Are you now? Well, I aim to please." His hands settle back on my hips. "You know the moment that I was first attracted to you?" he asks.

"On the steps of your house?"

"I mean really attracted to you. The real Vesper Smith, not just your long legs and blonde hair."

I swat him for parroting back what I said, and he catches my arms and puts them around his neck. I press my boobs into him and it feels so good. So right.

"The first time you were attracted to me," I muse.

"When you told everyone that my name meant 'God' in Greek."

"After which you called me a nerd so everyone would laugh at me."

He winces. "Not my finest moment."

"No, but I forgive you." I'm buoyant in Theo's arms. My feet still touch the bottom of the pool, just barely. We're dancing in the water, rocking around and around, twirling slowly in the water. Everything about Theo makes me feel young and giddy. Like a first crush, and I really am a virgin. Maybe that's his power. He makes you feel brand new.

"Your turn," he says. "Tell me about the first time you saw me, the real me."

"The skate park," I say. "The way you talked to those kids. Treated them like equals."

Theo draws me deeper into the pool.

He undoes my ponytail and my hair spreads out across the water, a golden waterfall.

"After which I yelled at you. I really am an asshole."

"No. You were protecting those kids, as well as yourself. You're a good guy."

"No, I'm not. I'm bad. Very, very bad."

"How bad?"

He lifts me. My legs automatically wrap around his hips. I'm ready to slide my pussy up and down those washboard abs.

Then he pulls me off and tosses me into the water.

"You punk," I shriek when I come up for air.

"Very, very bad." He smirks.

I swim and pretend fight him. He's too big and too strong and wrestles me so my back is at his front.

"Let me go," I try to elbow him and he holds me fast.

"Say the magic word."

"Please."

"That's not the magic word." His lips find my pulse and he kisses and licks before sucking hard enough to leave a hickey.

"Argh," I thrash, try to stomp on his foot and he only lifts me, carries me easily to shallow water. I pant. My bikini top is about to fall off. I tell him this and his deep, vibrating chuckle almost makes me cum.

He holds my hands crossed in front of me. Bends me over a bit. His weapon is poking between my legs.

"Beg me to fuck you."

His cock slides along the seam of my pussy, and the bikini does nothing to protect me. Little sparks of pleasure fly through me.

"Please," I whisper instead.

"You're going to beg a lot tonight," he promises, and runs his tongue along my ear.

He lets me go, but things have changed, we circle each other like the moon and sun, unable to resist the gravitational pull.

Drops of water bead on his tattooed shoulders. I want to lick them off. Instead I run my hand along the bunched muscle.

He scoops me up in his arms again. I run a thumb along his perfect lips, feel his cock press into my belly.

"Everyone has secrets," I whisper. "Everyone has a dark side. But not you. You wear your sins on your sleeve. Your secret, your dark side is that you're a good guy. What's it like to live like that? Completely honest?"

"V," he whispers. But I never learn what he wanted to say because when I tilt my face to his, he kisses me.

Theo knows what to do with his lips and tongue. I'm lost in him.

He carries me out of the pool, past the table, into the hall where he sets me down long enough to grab a white towel and wrap it around me.

My arms are threaded around his neck and I don't let go.

"Theo—"

"Bed. Now." He lifts me again, starting back to the penthouse.

We make it as far as the hall.

My skin is cold from the water, and I need to rub myself against him. His body warms me, igniting me. I kiss him fiercely, cupping his face to hold him still.

He lifts me and presses me to the wall.

My pussy throbbing like a second heartbeat, beating with a rhythm that belongs to him. Only him.

His fingers find my folds and slide up and down, spreading my wetness over my slit.

"Condom," I gasp, before I lose my mind completely.

He nods absently sets me down and drops to his knees.

His mouth covers my labia, warm and shocking. His lips and tongue repeat their clever activity. Apparently kissing my mouth was just practice. Mouth sealed to my pussy, he makes out with me like he means it. His hands prop up my bottom, and as his tongue enters me my shoulders practically crawl up the wall.

"Oh God," I'm moaning, my head flung back. "Oh God."

Theo tongue fucks me to orgasm as I'm plastered to the wall, holding onto his dark hair for dear life.

When he lets me down, I start to slide all the way to the floor. Instead he catches me in his arms and heads for the elevator. It's all fun and games and intense making out until the doors open with a ping and I realize we're almost at his penthouse.

I duck my head against his chest. "The security guards. Fuck. I can't have Evans see me like this."

"Relax, baby. I cleared the top floor. No one's up here," he confirms my guess. He opens the door one handed and carries me in. "I want to take you in every hallway, on every surface, in every room of this place. I've been dying to get inside you since you turned up in the ridiculous suit, and then cat walked to the pool in a bikini and put me in my place."

I laugh, giddy.

"You're a bad girl, Vesper. Tempting me. Teasing me."

He sets me down. "Get on the bed."

I lean over it, shake my bikini clad ass in his direction.

He smacks it, hard.

"Up."

I crawl onto it on all fours, waving my ass in the air. "Like this?"

"Yes. Now stay like that." He peels the wet fabric of my bikini down and seals his mouth between my bottom cheeks. I squeal as he rims me. Too hot. Too dirty. Too much.

"Feel good?" he asks.

"No," I protest, and he proves me wrong when he does it again, stroking my wet folds at the same time.

This time I protest when he pulls away.

"This is mine tonight. He grabs ahold of my right bottom cheek and squeezes before smacking it again, hard. "I'm going to fuck you anyway I want. And Vesper? I want it all."

Arousal boils through me. Pleasure already spiking in my nipples, my pussy, my bottom where he spanked me.

"Put your hand between your legs. Get yourself off."

I lean forward, spread my knees, give him a show. My orgasm dances just out of reach. I chase it with my fingers, panting, writhing. My breasts break free from the bikini top. I arch further, letting my nipples chafe against the bed.

"Stop," he orders. His tongue rims my asshole again. Sensation licks through me, taboo and perfect. So right. So, so right. So very, very wrong.

A tremor goes through me, a foreshadow of ecstasy. I moan, loud and low.

"Fuck." He spanks me again. "You're such a dirty girl. Keep touching yourself but don't cum."

My whole body rocks, as I fuck my hand.

"Do not cum," he warns as my legs shake. His words drive me higher. "Beg me for it."

"Please."

"No," he pulls my hand away. "I want you desperate. You only cum when I'm inside you tonight."

Shaking with need, I follow as he tugs on my hair. He pulls me around to where he kneels on the bed, his cock bobbing in front of my face.

"Yes," I breathe before diving forward to swallow him down. I tongue the vein on the underside his cock as my mouth engulfs him, moaning around his delicious length. He grips my hair controlling me. I fucking love it.

He's close when he guides me off his cock. "Not in your mouth." He props me in position, on my back, knees wide.

He hooks my legs in the crook of his elbows, and rams into me. One thrust and he's balls deep. My supreme arousal means I'm ready, but I cry out at the delicious feeling. His cock is long enough to hit the back of my womb and thick enough to rub all the lovely points in between.

He slides out, almost all the way, and waits a beat before slamming into me. The force batters my clit, smacking it awake. I cry out in happy surprise and catch his shoulders, hanging on for dear life, as he does it again, pulling out and slamming home. One more time, my orgasm detonates like a bomb.

Theo props my legs up over his shoulders as he drives in powerfully. Dragging me to the edge of orgasm again. I claw his arms and he growls like an animal.

It's raw and brutal and beautiful.

"Touch yourself," he demands.

I slip my hand between us and find my clit, but it's too much sensation, and I tell him.

He grabs my ankles, holding my legs straight up as he pounds away.

"Look at me. Fucking you hard. You want my cum?"

"Yes, fuck, yes."

"Yeah? Play with your breasts. Give me a good show, Vesper. Be my bad girl."

I cup my breasts, pinching my nipples. "I want you," I breathe. "I want you to cum."

"You're such a bad girl."

"I'm so bad. So very, very bad."

My pussy tightens with an impending orgasm. It blows up around me, catching me off guard. My inner muscles squeeze like a fist around his cock.

"Oh, fuck me." He falls forward, onto his hands, bucking and shuddering as he cums.

I pull him to me as he catches his breath. Before I know it, he's pulling out, and moving me again, propping me on all fours.

"Again?" I ask, surprised, as Theo comes at me with his cock hard and stiff as a spear.

"Again."

THREE ROUNDS LATER, I'm curled limp on the duvet. Theo lowers my leg from where he propped it to take me from behind. He rises to take care of the condom. When he returns he tucks close, kissing the back of my neck.

"She was right," I murmur. "You are a god."

He chuckles.

"Does this make me a goddess?"

"Oh yes," he nestles me further into his arms. "I will build a temple to you and worship every day."

"Mmmm," I purr. "You know, your house is serious Greek revival."

He shudders. "My dad. He collected the classical stuff. Apparently, mom liked it. Reminded her of home."

"I can't believe you're the crown prince of Sweden."

"I can't believe it myself. I just want to be a normal guy, you know."

I turn and kiss him. "You just fucked me three times in a row, and made me cum each time. We've past normal territory. You really are a god."

We doze a little when a popping sound outside makes me stir.

"What's that?"

"A surprise. Come on."

When he leads me back up to the pool, I almost pull away, but the sight of fireworks exploding above the park has me rushing to the railing. "Oh my god." The whistling rockets fly up and burst into the night in a shower of colored sparks.

"You did this?" I turn to him. "For me?"

He shrugs.

I don't know what to say. As far as I know, he's never

pulled a stunt like this to get a girl into bed. Not that he'd have to.

"Thank you."

We stand and watch them together, me leaning back into Theo. The sheet dips scandalously low. I don't care. When the grand finale starts, I turn, press my bare boobs against his chest, and kiss him.

MORNING FINDS us in his penthouse, our legs tangled together.

He wakes and smiles at me. I almost reach for my glasses, but I realize I don't have them. "Hey."

"Hey," he says as I climb out of bed. I don't want to go. Sleepy Theo blinking in the morning light is adorable.

"Come back to bed," he groans and tries to catch my arm. I skip out of the way.

"I can't. You have an interview today. We have to get ready."

"Don't wanna get ready. Wanna fuck."

"Get out of bed now and I'll let you fuck me in the shower."

I'm halfway to the bathroom when he practically body slams me, tossing me up over his shoulder, silencing my yelp with a smack to my ass.

Under the spray, he slides his hands all over my body, slippery with soap. He turns me around and cocks my leg up on the edge of the tub, easing his way inside.

"These are so beautiful," he breathes in my ear, fondling my breasts. "I want to cum on them. I want you to wear my cum all day, under that professional suit of yours."

"Mmm." I reach back and hold on to his neck as he fills me beautifully.

His teeth find my shoulder and he nips. I yelp, and he soothes the spot with his tongue.

"I'm sorry, baby. I want to mark you all over. I want everyone to know you're mine."

That does it. I cum around his cock, palms pressed to the tile, moans echoing around the bath.

"THERE SHE IS. IN HER SUIT," Theo murmurs as I come out dressed to take on the day. I spent the last ten minutes painting makeup over the hickey he gave me.

"You," I point at him, "are very, very bad."

"Me?" He bats his long lashes, all innocence. "I was seduced by a very bad—"

I push against his chest and kiss him.

"What was that?" I ask once I pull away.

"No comment."

"Good boy. I have to go check in with Evans. Meet you here in one hour. Okay?" I pause at the door. "No running. No commandeering a hot rod to joyride through Manhattan. And, for the love of all things proper, keep your shirt on."

"If I do, what's in it for me?"

"I'll let you cum on me. While wearing the suit." I pose against the door. His eyes light.

"And Theo? If you're really, really good... I'll wear the glasses."

I head to the suite Evans commandeered for an office. The head of security stalks over when I walk in, looming over me.

"Everything good? I haven't had time to check my phone —" I stop talking when I see his face.

"I hired you to fix the problem. Not make it worse," He throws a stack of paper in my face. They fall in heavy whipping sounds, not paper at all. Huge glossy photographs. Of Theo. Of me. The pool, and us the railing. The kiss in the light of the fireworks. Theo's arms are wrapped around me, but it's obvious I'm not wearing a shirt.

Shit.

"It's all over the news. Theo caught with his pants down, again. That's not all," his face is so red it's almost purple. "They're saying you used to be an escort. That you did it all through college."

"What?" I whisper, gathering up the glossies and holding them to my chest, a very fragile armor.

"Is it true? Who the hell are you, Vesper Smith?"

"I can fix this," I say shakily. I go to push my glasses up my face, but they're gone.

"I don't wanna hear it. You're fucking fired."

"I'm sorry—"

"Get out," Evans hisses. "Get your things and get out."

THE WALK back to Theo's room is the longest of my life. My phone shakes with Google alerts. "Crown prince caught with escort." The scenario is happening, resurrected from my nightmares. Everything I tried to fix. Everything I tried to hide. Out in the open.

Even when I was an escort I never felt shame like this. Back then, I was so focused. Each client brought me closer to becoming a college graduate. A business woman. Someone Miss Mavery would be proud of.

I got my degree and the contacts to launch my career, but it came at a price. I thought I paid it.

Turns out I still owed, and it would cost me everything I'd built. But if I was very, very lucky, it wouldn't cost me the man I was falling in love with.

I open the door to the penthouse and walked in without really seeing anything. "Theo, I—"

I stop at the giggle. Theo stood there, with blondie. She's dressed in a tight grey skirt, blouse and jacket, laughing as she fixes Theo's shirt collar.

Long legs, blonde hair. Grey suit.

Guess I've been replaced.

"Vesper?" Theo says. The blonde goes to touch him and he jerks away.

A little too late. "What's wrong?"

"Are you fucking kidding me?" I blurt.

Blondie smirks at me. "Theo," she reaches for him, and though he pushes her away, my stomach churns with betrayal.

"Never mind. I'm sorry. I'm sorry I interrupted. I'm sorry —for everything." I turn for the door. This time I don't see my way clearly because my vision fills with tears.

"Vesper," Theo shouts this time, but I pick up my pace, and flee.

7

"I'm sorry," Mina says, the regret in her voice clear even through the phone. "I thought I'd buried it deep enough."

"It's okay. Secrets always come out," I say wearily. It's a sentiment I tell my clients, and it chafes my ears. "I wonder who talked?" I throw my things in the suitcase.

"I've done some digging. Rumor has it one of Theo's hang arounds is an escort too."

"Of course. Betrayed by one of my own."

"You're not—" Mina makes a noise in frustrated. "Look, you were an escort. So what? It's perfectly legal."

"What I did in hotel rooms was not," I said.

"It put you through school," she continues. Mina is nothing if not stubborn. "It's not something to be ashamed of."

"Yet, here I am," I say, weary. "Ashamed. The first guy I've liked in years, and I ruined it."

Mina says nothing. I hear her struggling to think of something nice to say, and then she gives up. "Shit."

"Yeah." I throw the last of my things into my suitcase and

zip it up. The hotel room is pristine. Once I leave, it'll be like I was never even here.

The hickey on my neck throbs. *I want to mark you.* And he did. My pussy still aches for him.

Oh Vesper, you sure can pick 'em.

"Shit," Mina repeats.

"I know, I really fucked things up—"

"No, not that. I mean, you did, but—"

"Well, thanks. Next time you want to make me feel better, just don't—"

"He's on TV," Mina interrupts.

"What?"

"He's standing outside the hotel and talking to the press." She squeals. "Oh my god! You have to see this. Channel 108."

I rush to turn on the TV. Theo stands in front of his hotel, painted by camera flashes.

"I know my reputation isn't at its best," he says. His hair is mussed and his shirt rumpled, the stark white setting off his tanned skin. He looks dashing. "For too long I've put off my responsibilities. I have a lot to make right. But, a few days ago, I met someone." He pauses, a faraway smile on his face. "She showed me I'm more than my reputation. She challenged me to be more. If she's listening now, I'd like to make her a promise. I will clean up my act. Vesper, if you'll come back to me, I'll make it right."

"Oh fuck," I say, as Theo nods and leaves, the press still shouting for more.

"Oh fuck!" Mina squeals. "Isn't that the most romantic shit you ever saw? Maybe I won't form an investor group to short his company's stock and send it into a death spiral."

She blathers on about her plans of revenge which, knowing her, are barely legal.

"Mina!" I finally interrupt.

"What?"

"Where is he?"

"How would I know?"

"Mina."

"Heh, you're right. I hacked his phone, as soon as I knew you were hot for him. You know he's gotten some texts from Pepper Spice? He blocked her number."

"Mina, where is he?"

"One sec." There's a long pause and I rub my forehead. Not even vodka and Valium will touch this headache. "He's still at the hotel."

"You sure?" The clock reads almost ten. "He should be on his way to his interview by now."

"Well, I only can tell you where his phone is—"

"Vesper?" Comes a muffled voice, followed by banging on the door.

"I've got to go," I tell Mina, before running to open the door. Theo bursts in. His big body crowds me back.

"Theo, what are you doing? You're missing your interview."

"Fuck the interview," he pulls me into his arms. "I don't want to talk to those people. I want to be with you. You're the only one who sees me."

His mouth claims mine, lighting me up with an electric kiss.

I break it off, even though it physically hurts to do it.

"You can't be here," I say to his throat. "You can't be seen with me."

"Because you were an escort?"

"Yes—"

"I don't care." He kisses me again, separating only to murmur. "I don't care about any of that."

I should protest, but his desire inflames mine, and sweeps all thought away. I cling to him as he lifts me, his large hands cupping my ass as we walk to the bed.

"I want you," he breathes, wild-eyed. I nod. He yanks down his pants and produces a condom from his pocket as I shuck my own clothes. As soon as he rolls it on he sits on the bed and I straddle him, sinking slowly onto his thick staff. Once he's sheathed inside me, my hips rock, my mind blanking as I ride him. He holds me gently, supporting me until pleasure rolls through me, gentle as an ebbing tide.

I gasp, calling his name.

"My turn," he growls, and grips my hips. I cry out as he drives into me. My breasts bob up and down as I bounce on his cock.

"Fuck, Vesper, fuck," he chants. His fingers bite into my ass. I hang onto his shoulders, feeling his marble hard muscles bunch and tighten under my hands.

His cock hits a pleasure spot deep inside of me, and I jerk out of control, bucking with my orgasm.

With a curse, he thrusts upwards, body taut as he cums.

We collapse back on the bed.

"That was—" I gasp, and shake my head, unable to finish.

"Yeah," he agrees. We both laugh.

"No comment," I say, but my humor dies.

I sit up. "I should go."

"No." Theo reaches for me and I shake him off, grabbing up my pants. "That was a nice fuck but—"

"Stop," he orders, and I do. "Vesper. This is not goodbye."

"No?" I go to touch my glasses, and when they're not there, I push back my hair instead.

"I'm not." He shakes his head. "I'm not ready for goodbye."

"You were this morning, with blondie."

"Who? Oh, you mean Nessa?"

"Yes, Nessa," I spit. "Why was she in the bedroom with you?"

Theo's brows knit together, which only makes me madder. He doesn't get to be indignant. Not about this. "Fuck if I know. She said you and Evans sent her to help me get ready for the interview."

"Oh, I'm so sure," I snarl. "Did she fluff you before you slept with Pepper Spice, too?"

"What the fuck?"

"You. Are. A. Slut," I scream. "You're a crown prince who's slept with roughly half the women on the planet. At least three of whom have been caught on camera. Me included." I sag onto the bed, my anger passing like a summer storm. "I can't believe I was so stupid. I can pick them." I cover my face with my hands. Forget glasses. I'm going to have to wear a bag over my head for the rest of my life.

Theo closes his hands around mine and draws them down. "Vesper, stop." He kneels before me. "Don't be hard on yourself. You're right. I don't deserve you. Please." He kisses my hand. "Please just give me a chance."

"It's not going to work. The press is right. I was an escort before I got my degree. That private club I told you about? That's where I met my clients. One of them got me my first internship that turned into a job."

"Vesper, I don't care."

"The world does. The board of your father's company does. I bet your grandmother does. You can't just stride into Sweden with me on your arm. It doesn't work like that." My throat burns from holding back tears. "I'm sorry I lied to you."

"I'm sorry. If it wasn't for me, they wouldn't have dug it up." He threads his fingers through mine. "You told me everyone has secrets. We're probably the only two people in the world with none."

"I made my bed." The words come out hollow. "I'm going to lie in it."

He rises and stretches out beside me, drawing me down onto the coverlet. "Lie in it then. With me."

"What do you mean?"

"We don't have to deal with any of this. It's bullshit. I don't care what these people think of me. I care what you think. And you're right. I have enough wealth, and enough of a platform, I can do something. I can make a difference." He kisses my hand again. "Help me."

"Theo." Now my throat clogs. "I should've asked you from the beginning, day one that I started working for you. What do you want? I can make Theo Kensington. But who do you want to be?"

He closes his eyes. Opens them. "I want to be happy," he says. "I want to be free."

"Paint the picture for me. Let me see it."

"I want to get up in the morning and do something that matters. I want to skateboard on the weekends. And come home to a beautiful woman." He caresses my cheek.

"Beautiful, intelligent woman," I correct.

He rolls on top of me. "Beautiful, intelligent woman." He punctuates each word with a kiss. "Stay with me, Vesper. I don't know what I'm going to do about the board, and the queen, but I don't care. I want you."

We get distracted for a few minutes, and then my phone rings. Out of habit I look for it. Theo, gentleman that he is, grabs it for me. "Evans," he grimaces, and answers it. "You're fired." He tosses the phone on the bed and climbs back to me.

"What was that?"

"He sent Nessa to me. I just know it. Maybe he wanted to deflect attention from you, or, I don't know."

I ponder this as he slides me back into his arms. "I think I know what to do about the board."

"Really?"

"Yeah. Resign."

He stares at me.

"You don't want to be on the board? Don't be on the board. You still have a majority stake in the company. Your vote has weight."

His shoulders slump. "It's my father's legacy. I can't let him down."

"Your father made himself. I bet he'd want you to be your own man. Besides, he didn't build his company for you. He built it for her. To prove he was good enough for a princess."

After a moment, Theo nods. "You're right."

"Send them a letter of resignation. Bow out quietly. Tell them you want to focus on your volunteer efforts. Which is true. If in a few years you change your mind, you can petition for reinstatement."

A slow smile spreads across his face. "You gonna solve all my life's problems for me, smart girl?"

"Probably," I answer. "Give me a few minutes." We laugh.

"What about Sweden?" he asks.

"What do you want to do about Sweden?"

"You think I can get away with blowing off an audience with a queen?"

"I wouldn't advise it. But what do you want?"

"I want to go," he says after a pause. "It would mean a lot to my mother, if she was alive. I want to make peace with her family. For her."

"All righty then," I grab my phone and sit up. "Let's go see the queen."

~

ON HIS PRIVATE PLANE, Theo lounges beside me, worrying the long sleeves of his dress shirt. He rolled them up just enough to show the black edges of one tattoo. Miss Mavery would make him wear it properly, but I think he looks hot.

He slides down in his seat, long legs splayed. I flick his thigh.

"Ow."

"The queen will not appreciate your man spread."

"Fucking A."

"Or cursing. Or slouching."

"All right, all right," he sits up. "Motherfucking Henry Higgins around here."

"I know that reference. Watch it." I waggle a finger before opening my laptop to check on things. My stomach still clenches at the thought of checking social media, so I go straight to my email. There's one from Mina with only the message: "*007 requesting contact.*"

"Can I make a phone call?" I move to the seat with the phone near it. The stewardess helps me dial out. Mina answers on the first ring.

"I took the liberty of contacting some of your old friends. Well, your old clients. I don't know if you'd call them friends."

My stomach plummets to my knees. "You didn't."

"Yes, and they were very interested in keeping your reputation intact. They like to keep things private, as you know."

"You didn't," I repeat, feeling sick and giddy at the same time, like I'm flying through the air without the airplane.

"The story is pretty much being hushed up. It's overshadowed by all the royal prince stuff, anyway. The spotlight won't swing again to you, and if it does, all the press will see is a beautiful woman who worked to put herself through college. The reports of you being an escort are greatly exaggerated. I mean, smart people will know, but you're not going to have people calling you a whore on national television. It's all wink, wink. Nod, nod. Hush, hush."

I clutch the edge of the seat, trying to make sense of her babbling.

"Are you okay?" Theo mouths at me.

I nod, not sure whether I should cry or whoop with triumph. Calling my old clients is a bold move, but Mina's right. A lot of them are very powerful, and still care for me. I would never reach out to them, so Mina did it for me.

I could cry, she's such a good friend.

I also could kill her.

Mina is still prattling on. "I'm not sure we can destigmatize sex work with one press conference, so it's the best I could do. Honestly, V, you should be fine. You're going to Amsterdam, right?"

"Sweden."

"Close enough. I mean all those European countries are so close together. Holland to Sweden is like me driving to New Jersey—and they don't have a problem with sex work like we do in America. In Holland, I mean, not New Jersey. Not that you were a sex worker, but we all know what escorts really do—"

"Mina," I cut in. "Thank you. What you did was genius. Just, please, stop trying to make me feel better."

Mina blows into the phone as she sighs in relief. "Thank, fuck. This empathetic shit is hard."

"I really appreciate it."

"Let me know what else I can do. I'm on standby, ready to destroy your enemies."

"That won't be necessary."

"Well, if it is, I'll be all over it. I'm here for ya." We say goodbye and she hangs up.

I set the phone down, my hand trembling a little.

"Vesper?" Theo watches me, concerned.

"It's handled," I whisper, and clear my throat. "My past. My reputation. We've done as much damage control as we can do. It's handled."

"Do I want to know how?"

"No." I press my fingers to my lips, wishing I could hold everything in. "But I'll tell you if you want."

He slides from his seat and comes to sit beside me. "It doesn't matter." He takes my hand and kisses it. He's been doing that a lot.

Maybe a playboy can turn into Prince Charming.

THEO KEEPS a hand on my back as we walk into the Stockholm palace. The massive building is the official royal residence.

"There are three floors and fourteen thousand and thirty rooms," our guide intones. "Done in a Baroque style."

As we walk through the gilded rooms, I catch a glimpse of a nymph statue, cavorting under the grim stare of some important Swedish dude's portrait. Looks familiar.

"This place is gorgeous," I whisper. "I can't imagine ever wanting to leave."

"Stockholm syndrome," he says with a completely straight face.

I'd elbow him in the ribs, but I don't want to get beheaded for assaulting a prince. Theo and I spent all night researching as much as we can about royal protocol. We only got through several centuries worth, but I'm confident we can get through this royal audience without a major gaffe, like starting a war.

I hope.

The guide leaves us in a room with vaulted ceilings and polished parquet floors.

"Nervous?" I whisper.

He answers with a huff that could be 'yes' or 'no'.

"You'll be fine. You look so handsome." And he does.

The doors open. We both turn as an entourage enters, led by a steely-haired woman with dark eyes.

"Grandmother," he bows.

"Theodore," she says in perfect English, with a slight British accent, and offers her cheek. He kisses it lightly. There's no hug or warm greetings, but it's okay. It's a start.

Theo steps aside and draws me forward. "Allow me to present my media specialist and the smartest woman I know. Vesper Smith, my girlfriend."

The queen raises an eyebrow, looking like her grandson, except for a poker face that would make Miss Mavery proud.

"How do you do," I curtsey to the queen.

Her eyes narrow.

This is it. The next words out of her mouth will either accept me or make it clear I'm not welcome.

Theo's hand tightens around mine. *I'm not going to let you go,* he told me. Nothing matters, as long as we're together.

"So this is the woman who brought my grandson back to me."

"Yes, grandmother. I wouldn't be here without Vesper. She convinced me we should meet and have a relationship. I'd like to try."

"It has been too long. Far too long, and entirely my fault. When your mother left, I listened to my advisors. They told me to cut her off, to retain the respect of the realm. I did so, and it was a balm for my hurt pride." Her voice drops. "What I wouldn't give to go back and do it differently."

"Grandmother," Theo says in a gentle tone he'd started to use more and more.

"There's nothing for it. We must make amends while we can. Life is very short. You look so much like your mother." Theo takes the queen's hand and squeezes it. Are there tears glittering in the monarch's eyes?

The queen clears her throat, becoming imposingly regal once more, but Theo keeps his tender expression.

"As for swaying public opinion, maybe your girlfriend will have some ideas about that."

"I'm sure she does," Theo says. "She's brilliant."

Queen and prince turn to me, with matching smiles.

Ms. Mavery, if you could see me now.

EPILOGUE

Two years later...

"We're going to be late," I say, breathless.

"I don't care. I never did stand on ceremony." Theo grips my hand tighter.

We rush past the paintings of solemn Swedish kings. After two years of regular visits to the palace, I can name almost all of them now.

"In here." Theo pulls me into an alcove. Gold leaf glitters in the wallpaper, but it's pretty modestly decorated overall. At least there aren't nymphs romping. Not that there need be. Theo has made it his life's mission to chase me down each and every hall after hours and have his way with me. I still get a thrill whenever I see an original Klimt hanging in the Gold room. Theo did things to me under the famous painting that would make a porn star blush.

My dress twitches up. I whirl and smack his hand. "Not now. There are people around. Tourists!"

"Not today. They cleared the place out for the wedding. I've always wanted to do you here."

He kisses me, and I forget why I was arguing. While he distracts me with lips and tongue, he backs me against a divan.

"Right here," he growls, ripping off his tie. He turns me around and ties my hands behind my back. Heat bursts between my legs.

"Bend over." He tips me forward over the couch arm and tosses up the skirts of my dress.

"Fuck, is this for me?" He plays with the straps of my garter belt.

"No, it's for Anderson Cooper."

SMACK! His hand lands on my ass.

"Bad, bad girl. Pandering to the press again."

"You know it." I wriggle my bottom at him.

He teases me with the tip of his cock until I'm begging for it.

"You want this?"

"Mmm, yes."

"You sure? You gonna be a bad girl?"

"I'm your bad girl. But if you don't fuck me soon, we really are going to be late."

He spanks me a few more times, then thrusts inside.

Afterwards, I stand in front of a giant, gold framed mirror and fuss with my hair. With my golden braid and blue dress, I look like an ice princess.

We asked for a small wedding. Small turns out to be four hundred people, with another few thousand in attendance in the streets, waiting to see us. I scandalized everyone when I refused to wear white, but the queen backed down her disapproval when Theo threatened to show up shirtless.

We're not a typical royal couple, and I like it that way.

Theo stands beside me, straightening his tie. "I checked the news before I came," he says. "You're more popular than I am."

"Don't you forget it." I swat his arm.

"Careful, Mrs. Kensington," he says.

"You can't call me that," I protest. "Not yet. First you have to marry me."

"I'll call you whatever I want," he grips my bottom, hard and kisses me.

"You're looking quite handsome today, Prince Theo."

"And you look like a goddess."

"Maybe you need glasses."

"Maybe," he grins. We both know his corrective eye surgery went off without a hitch a year ago. "But I don't need to see to know how beautiful you are."

I flush.

He offers his arm. "Come on. Let's make you a princess."

The End

Want more smexy royal rom coms by Lee Savino? Click to read an excerpt from Royally Fake Fiancé

turn into dragons. The best part? The dragons insist I'm their mate.

Bad Boy Alphas with Renee Rose (bad boy werewolves)

Never ever date a werewolf.

ABOUT THE AUTHOR

Lee Savino has plans to take over the world, but most days can't find her keys or her phone, so she just stays home and writes smexy (smart + sexy) romance. She loves chocolate, lives in yoga pants, and looks great in hats.

For tons of crazy fun, join her Goddess Group on Facebook or visit www.leesavino.com to sign up for her mailing list and get a free book.

Website: www.leesavino.com
Facebook Goddess Group:
https://www.facebook.com/groups/LeeSavino/

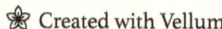